Little Abi

Show me a Place

SreeLatha Radhakrishnan

Ukiyoto Publishing

All global publishing rights are held by

Ukiyoto Publishing

Published in 2022

Content Copyright © SreeLatha Radhakrishnan

ISBN 9789364946407

All rights reserved.
No part of this publication may be reproduced, transmitted, or stored in a retrieval system, in any form by any means, electronic, mechanical, photocopying, recording or otherwise, without the prior permission of the publisher.

The moral rights of the author have been asserted.

This is a work of fiction. Names, characters, businesses, places, events, locales, and incidents are either the products of the author's imagination or used in a fictitious manner. Any resemblance to actual persons, living or dead, or actual events is purely coincidental.

This book is sold subject to the condition that it shall not by way of trade or otherwise, be lent, resold, hired out or otherwise circulated, without the publisher's prior consent, in any form of binding or cover other than that in which it is published.

www.ukiyoto.com

In celebration of the triumphs and resilience of children everywhere.

CONTENTS

Camp School	1
Memories of Life Back Home	3
Mirfat	6
A Hard Life Ahead	8
The Desperate Journey	11
A Safe Haven	14
What About My Friends?	16
About the Author	*19*

Camp School

"Hurry up amma, I am going to be late. I will have to sit right at the back and then I can hardly see the teacher or the blackboard". cried Abi, while amma handed her daughter a plastic lunch box. Abi adjusted her long black hair that was neatly braided all the way down to her waist. Her bright, round face glowed in the reflection of her smock and Abi took a quick look at the mirror. She was nine years old, but still not as tall as her friend Ameena.

Abi grabbed the lunch box, stood thinking for a minute and opened it expertly. Abi took a quick whiff and made a face." Noodles again ! I am so fed up with the same lunch day after day. I will exchange it with

Ameena. She has promised to bring kebabs today. Her father managed to get some meat and potatoes from a vendor yesterday." Amma smiled sadly as she grabbed little Abraham who was clinging to his sister's skirt. Abi let go of the little one's hand and ran fast to reach the school at the other end of the huge refugee camp in which she lived.

All along the way she wiped away her tears that came streaming down her tiny face. She knew that her mother was doing her best under the circumstances and Abi had been rude to her. She had seen amma's sad face from the corner of her eye and now she felt sorry for her. She remembered the lovely lunch box amma prepared for her back home. Each day brought new surprises-falafel, cakes, meat balls and chicken cutlets. She loved to open her neatly packed food slowly in front of her friends. The girls went on a sharing spree grabbing each other's lunch and enjoying every morsel of their mothers' love packed into those neat boxes. The war had changed everything-her food, her mood and her lifestyle.

Abi reached the make-shift school just in time to get a place next to Ameena. Her dear friend Ameena was the only one who got to stay in the same camp as Abi. The others were shuffled around and placed in different camps elsewhere. Some of them had managed to flee to European countries with the help of friends and relatives who had already settled there. The teacher was less grumpy today-probably she had got a good meal for herself and her family. She cracked a few jokes before she started her class and then plunged headlong into fractions, square root and equations one after the other. Abi and Ameena could hardly keep pace with the speed of the math session, but they knew fully well that the teacher had to finish quickly, go back to her tent, feed her children and come back to teach the students in the afternoon shift. There were so many children that the camp authorities had to split them into two sessions – a seven- to -one morning shift followed closely by a one-thirty -to- six afternoon shift.

Abi and Ameena strolled back hand -in-hand after class. They talked longingly about their life before the war, as Abi munched softly on the kebabs that Ameena had brought for her and let the juice from the meat sink slowly inside. "I wonder if our school building was bombed too?" wondered Ameena loudly." I heard amma's friends say that a fire destroyed half the front portion of the main school and the rest simply crumbled down soon afterwards," said Abi in a soft whisper.

Memories of Life Back Home

The girls could never forget their old school back home. The main building stood tall and majestic with the Principal's office and the nurse's station. Right behind was the grand auditorium that had seen so many children showcasing their talents. Abi remembered rehearsing in front of the mirror several times before her annual day function. She was in a musical show and was chosen to be the lead singer. The lights, the heavy satin curtains, and the orchestra had set her head spinning in spite of many rehearsals. But her performance was so wonderful that the audience went on to cheer her on for hours. Her parents and family clapped so loudly that little Abi blushed in embarrassment.

The auditorium was connected to another row of tall, brick buildings with huge trees all around and neat classrooms painted in bright colours. Abi's school was just a hop-step-jump away from her home and she could even get a glimpse of amma's purple hydrangea blooms from her playground. Little Abraham would run along with her half-way clinging to the navy blue lunch bag that Amma had specially designed for her. Abi loved school because of her friends.. There was Sada, Ameena, Maya and Leila. They were a close-knit gang and often got into trouble for chattering too much or giggling when the class was going on. Once Ameena tied Maria's plait to the desk and everyone burst out laughing when Maria struggled to get up. Miss Suraiya, the class teacher, was furious. Abi and her friends went to detention, of course. But Abi enjoyed that too, because she got to stay longer with her friends. Luckily, papa never got to hear about it at the parent-teacher meeting.

Another day, the girls were straddling home after an early break when they saw Jared, the old boatman standing near the huge lake facing the school. They eyed the old boatman with his weary smile and waved cheerily to him. The girls always wanted to go on a boat ride all by themselves. "Don't even think about it," Papa had said, when Abi suggested the idea to her father. "YOU are not to get into the boat without an adult by your side. The currents are not predictable and you are not a great swimmer either. The water gets deeper and deeper as you move into the centre of the lake." Abi's papa explained all the details as he knew that Abi would come up with a lot of questions soon after his long lecture. But somehow, the boatman standing idle was a serious temptation for the girls. Without thinking much, they bargained with old Jared and pooled in some money to pay for the fare. They begged him to take them for a small ride. The boatman was hesitant at first because there were no adults to accompany the girls. Finally, when he saw the disappointed little faces, he agreed and asked the girls to get in. He did not realize that the girls with their school bags made a heavy cargo and very soon the boat started to wobble. The girls thought it was all a part of the adventure, and started munching on their snacks. The sun was shining brightly, the open blue sky was an absolute dream and the emerald green waters ran so close to them that they could trail their hands in the water. The girls splashed the icy cold droplets across each other and were screaming and shouting, when all of a sudden the boat capsized and the girls tumbled into the water even before they knew what hit them. None of them knew swimming and the boatman was too old and feeble to get hold of them. Luckily, two or three fishermen saw the accident, rushed to their rescue and brought them to the shore in a matter of minutes. Drenched from head to toe and gasping for breath, the girls were crying and hugging each other as their parents ran to fetch them after hearing the news. Feeling terribly scared and guilty for not heeding their parents' advice, the girls rushed home sheepishly with what remained of their bags and books. They were all grounded for a week but the girls often chuckled about it later in the school playground. They shuddered to think what might have happened if the fishermen had not been around. One good thing that came out of all this, was that the girls started attending swimming classes in earnest.

Abi and Ameena were so lost in their past, that they lost track of time. They knew that they had to hurry back to the camp before dusk, lest their parents got worried.

"Will we ever get to see our dear friends? I wonder where they are?" mused Ameena, as they started walking briskly, while Abi stared sadly into the empty space tears brimming up every now and then. She had begged amma and papa to get some information of their friends' whereabouts but nobody seemed to know the finer details and there was no way to trace them.

Mirfat

Whenever Abi thought about her life before the war, her heart raced wildly with a yearning that nearly tore her apart. Her life had been so simple, so precious. Her father had a steady job as a lab technician in a hospital nearby. They had a comfortable home and Abi always dreamt of living in the same house for years to come. The garden was amma's haven. She planted lovely aromatic herbs on one side and vegetables and olives at the rear end. There were beautiful flowers that welcomed visitors in the patio area and the compound was lined with thick bushes. Cuckoos and kingfishers would sneak in and out quietly while Abi watched quietly through her blue and white curtains. A row of comic books and delicate figurines were lined up neatly near the window. Papa had painted the roof with stars and planets with a huge moon in the centre. When the lights went off, the glow from the ceiling was simply magical. Ameena had loved the idea so much that she got her father to do up her room in the same way. Papa had made a swing for her on one of the trees and Abi and her friends spent many sunny days on it twirling this way and that, standing up and sitting down, pushing each other higher and higher squealing and screaming till their voices turned hoarse and shrill.

Abi's father worked as the chief lab technician in a hospital nearby. He loved his job and people always praised him for his kindness and politeness. Sometimes he was sent to people's homes to collect blood samples from patients who were too old to come to the clinic. He was very hard-working and very strict. Abi had to finish her homework, say her prayers and repeat her multiplication tables five times before she went out to play every day. She could not disturb anything in Papa's room as every object had a special place. But Abi could not help gazing at the huge map on the wall at least once every day. Papa was very ambitious for Abi and Abraham. He wanted Abi to become a doctor and work in the rural areas where medical facilities were very scarce. Abi loved the idea of wearing a coat and a stethescope and often went to the hospital with her father to watch patients being treated by the specialists there. She beamed with pride to see her father working tirelessly, saying soft,soothing words to the patients and their relatives.

At home her favourite past- time was to sit on the table in papa's office room and rotate the globe on the huge mahogany table. She would swing her legs back and forth and read the funny names of places all around the world-Addis Ababa, Djibouti, Minsk, Brussels, Azerbhaijan and so many, many others. She loved to imagine herself in all these places with her friends.She could see them all dressed up in native costumes running around the streets hand-in-hand. She would be lost in her own world till the aroma of Amma's delicious falafel and meat patties invited her to the kitchen," Don't touch anything till you wash your hands, you little imp," Amma would say with a twinkle in her eye. Amma's spacious living room with her hand- embroidered cushions and the soft silk diwans were such a welcome sight after a long day at school.

Mirfat, her baby pigeon, stood strutting around in her cage waiting to be fed. She always seemed hungry. Abi smiled to herself when she remembered how she found Mirfat. One day when Abi and Ameena were returning from school they found a fledgling fallen from a tree, fluttering its tiny wings and making feeble noises.Abi grabbed the helpless little thing and put it into her soft lunch bag. She brought it home with her, fed it water and milk from a tiny spoon and soothed it down. Ameena and she named the little one " Mirfat" in a heart beat. Mirfat had been the name of Abi's favourite parrot until an eagle had come scooping down on her one day. Abi had never ever got over that scene. So,when another winged visitor occupied the empty cage, Abi had been very happy.. The girls spent their holidays playing with the bird and enjoying its gentle cooing noises. Sometimes, even papa came over to see the new Mirfat's antics.

A Hard Life Ahead

But the war changed everything. There were bombs, guns, dust, blood and loud sirens. The old and the young were hurt badly and the sight of children without arms and legs seemed absolutely heart-rending. People were running here and there, packing, crying, holding each other, and before she even realized it Abi was whisked away to a camp along with many others. Mirfat too had to be left behind in all that confusion. When the war began, Papa told Abi that they could not take their bird with them as many camps did not allow pets. So Abi had to let go of her dear friend, very half – heartedly of course. Abi was worried if the delicate creature would be safe in the wild after having been raised as a pet. But to Abi's delight, just as they were leaving the house, she caught sight of her feathered friend sitting on one of window-sills nearby. Abi knew it was Mirfat because of the little black dot on her forehead. It seemed that Mirfat knew something was amiss and had come to say a special good-bye to her saviour. Abi's eyes filled with tears to see her dear Mirfat strutting around, confident in her new role as a strong survivor.

Abi and Ameena were lost in their own little world when suddenly, Abi's mother came running out and hurried the girls inside the camp. There was an announcement for rations, medicines and supplies of warm clothes and the girls had to stand in queue to along with their families before everything disappeared in the blink of an eye. Sometimes the lines were broken and people started grabbing stuff out of turn and there was a huge confusion afterwards. Abi was very tired but she knew how important it was to help her parents out in such situations. The rations were mostly soup, noodles, bread and potatoes. Abi felt nauseated at the thought of same kind of insipid menu. She tried to munch on the par boiled potatoes but some of them were so hard that she used them to play ball with the little kids around. She giggled so much when she pretended the beans were her Amma's sheekh kebabs and munched on them loudly, like grandma Selma's lazy, old goat, Miriam.

At the camp, papa quickly got a job in the hospital and was very, very busy. Amma helped people in any way that she could. She took care of babies while the mothers did their chores, taught sewing and embroidery to the young girls, and spoke kindly to the old and the ailing. She mended and patched up old clothes so beautifully that they looked better than they did before. Papa went on his bicycle to work and helped out in the blood collection department. Sometimes he worked two shifts, if there was a shortage of staff. Abi noticed that he was very tired but that he hardly complained." There are so many people who are worse than me. I consider myself blessed to be still able to work and earn for my family". Sometimes Amma gave him a mud pack massage and helped him stretch his legs in the cramped tent.

Winters were the worst. The blankets were never warm enough, and the heating never seemed to drive away the biting cold. Amma managed to get sweaters and shawls and covered up Abi and Abraham from head to toe. Sometimes papa helped to make huge fires along with the others to cheer up the long, sad faces of the people shivering inside the tents. Babies and old people were always falling sick and more than once Abi and papa had to rush patients to the emergency clinic for severe lung infections. Sometimes Abi had to close her ears to stop hearing the constant wheezing and coughing of sick people in the thick of winter. Summer was a relief in spite of the sudden rains that made the whole place slushy and dirty. At least they did not have to pile up layers and layers of clothes and watch a dreary,sky that seemed so dark and furious.

Abi and Ameena helped their parents a lot, before and after school. They hung up the clothes to dry, fetched food and rations, aired out their mattresses and played with their little brothers. The RED CROSS, UNICEF, DOCTORS WITHOUT BORDERS and many kind organisations arranged food, water, clothes, and medicines. Abi specially loved to watch the nurses and the doctors help the wounded and the sick. She often spoke about them to Ameena. "I wonder how they can be so patient and gracious in the midst of all this confusion. They must be missing their families and children too. How do they manage to stay away from their loved ones?" Ameena too did not have an answer to Abi's questions. Sometimes the volunteers brought pieces of chocolate for the children and showed them pictures and videos of their families in their lovely homes

Abi and Ameena often envied the peaceful life they were leading in their countries. "When will we ever get to smile like them? Will there be a time when we can ever go to a regular school or live in a house that has a proper bed and a warm bedcover?", the girls would ask each other and go into a dark, dirty, complaining mood for several hours. But somehow they learnt to snap out of it and accompany the volunteers handing out forms at the vaccination camps. They pretended to be grown-ups and cheered up the little ones who were afraid of injections. They drew cartoon figures on the plasters after the jabs and made funny faces to bring back a smile on the sad faces of the babies and toddlers. Some officials had taken down Abi's family details to see if they could speed up their process of migration to a European country like Germany or Swizerland. Abi begged them to include Ameena and her family too. The officials gave a warm smile and promised to do their best. "While you are waiting for your papers, learn some German and French. It will help you in your new school", said one of them to the girls. The two friends were so thrilled that they made up their minds to pay more attention to the foreign language classes taught in the camp school.

The Desperate Journey

One morning, papa came back a little earlier than usual and appeared to be very secretive and mysterious. He took Amma and Abi to a corner and told them that there was a group of refugees planning to go over to Germany. The journey was going to be tedious and dangerous. But papa had an air of confidence about him that made Abi very, very excited. Maybe this was the beginning of a new life, a proper school and a warm, safe home. The frequent bomb scares, the terrible news of more and more people dying in the camps and the mad scramble for rations and clothes had taken its toll on Abi and her parents. Abi hoped that she would not have to face the harsh weather anymore nor stand in long lines for water and food. She was so relieved to hear that Ameena's parents too were a part of this desperate mission.

"My experience as a senior technician will get me a job anywhere. I cannot go on living an empty dream. I need Abi and Abraham to make something out of their lives. I want a good education for them and a decent life for all of us," said papa. The new determination in papa's voice threw Abi off-gear. She had always seen papa wearing a troubled face whenever he set off on his bicycle. Ever since they moved to the refugee camp, papa had appeared to be gloomy and tired. But now he seemed like a different person- full of energy and cheer in the hope of a good future for his family and friends. "This is the best and probably the last opportunity to get out of this dreary life before I get too old or too sick", said papa. He knew he had to make a serious decision for the sake of his family.

In spite of a feeling of a mysterious journey ahead, Abi could not help feeling a little bit adventurous. The thought of Ameena and her family sharing the journey, made it even more action-packed.

The leader of the group held a meeting and spoke to them in very plain terms." Let me tell you from the very beginning that this is going to a very exhausting, perilous and expensive journey. There is a huge risk involved at every point of the journey and I do not want to hear any complaints at all. Here is a list of things that I want you to carry with you". The list included minimum luggage, important documents water and essentials.

Alarming as it sounded, there was no looking back and every one in the group went back to their tents, their faces drawn tight with a grim sense of determination.

The next day around midnight, the group were herded into a rickety bus about two kilometers away from the camp. The bus was pushed down the road for a mile or so, after which it picked up speed until it reached a point near the foothills of a steep mountain. The passengers were then quickly shifted to a train that was already packed like a tin of sardines. There were, huge hefty men at every point checking papers and ids. They carried rifles taller than them and looked very serious.. The darkness added to the secrecy and made everything look very frightening. Abi and Ameena held each other's cold, clammy hands and watched little Abraham fast asleep on amma's shoulders. The adults did not even dare to whisper.

After a scary journey through mountain passes and hilly terrain they reached flat ground. Abi could hear the sound of water lashing on the shore and realised they had reached a beach near a sea. Very quietly they were huddled into huge boats that were crowded with men, women and children. But the hope of a peaceful, stable life seemed to urge everybody to move quickly without asking too many questions. Each passenger was given a life vest and a bottle of water and a pill for sea-sickness. There was a deadly silence as the boats set to sail. After a few hours some of the passengers began feeling nauseous, the babies started crying while the mothers shushed them and rocked them to sleep. Sometimes the boats tossed around so much that it felt like an earthquake had hit them from under the sea. Abi swallowed her fear and anguish slowly as the boats spliced through the menacing blue and green waters. She and Ameena noticed that most of the people shut their eyes tight fearing the savage journey and the unknown destination ahead of them. As night appeared, the icy waters seemed to pierce through the skin and people started screaming and holding on to each other.

After about five hours of a harrowing voyage, suddenly as if by a strange miracle a huge ship was sighted and flares were sent from the boats to let the ship know of their presence. There were cries of relief and huge cheering as the ship approached them and soon everyone on the ship was taken to the shore. Luckily, the boats had reached friendly waters and they had reached a place where refugees were offered asylum by the local Government.

Each of the passengers was given a space blanket which shielded them from the cold temperatures and brisk winds and helped them retain their body heat. They were then transported to a temporary quarters, given a warm bed and a meal of thick bread slices, a piece of goat cheese and hot, steaming soup. They had been living on water and bits of chocolate for several hours and the hot meal was such a welcome relief.

A Safe Haven

The next day officials took them to a camp a few miles away."Oh no,not another camp," said Abi to Ameena and her parents. But papa scored again. While their papers were being sorted out,Papa's experience as a lab technician was taken into account and he and his family were reassigned to another line. Ameena's mother had been a senior nurse in the camp and so her family too got to join them. Abi was so relieved that she started crying and whimpering like a little baby. She could not take another moment of uncertainty.She wanted something permanent in her life. She would not stop till her mother cuddled her and soothed her down..After an initial wait of about two weeks, they were all packed into six or seven huge buses and given food packets, bottles of water and energy drinks. They had to travel another ten to twelve hours before they reached the German border,but this time the journey was more comfortable and most of the passengers went off into a deep, dreamless sleep, simply out of sheer relief and exhaustion. After a whole lot of formalities at the border they were again housed in huge buildings for a week. At last, after extensive paper work, a lot of questions and answers and a series of medical examinations, each family was assigned a small two bedroom apartment in a fairly decent locality. Abi and Ameena lived just two minutes away from each other and the girls were absolutely delirious with joy. There was a park and a playground nearby. The huge tress threw dark shadows all around and the girls were allowed to spend a few hours there every evening. It was nothing like home but there was peace, quiet and safety.

Soon the girls got to go to a school nearby.The teachers were kind and understanding and there were plenty of interpreters who helped the girls with the new language. Besides this,pictures, sign language,videos and language classes helped the girls mingle with the local students. Abi and Ameena got to meet boys and girls from other refugee camps and soon they were all jabbering nineteen to the dozen about their perilous journey, the new country they were going to live in and the new language that they were going to learn to speak and write in.

What About My Friends?

There was one thing that was disturbing Abi all day long. Miss Gunther, her guidance counsellor had been noticing a vacant look on Abi's face from time to time and was little concerned for her. One day she drew Abi aside and gently coaxed her into opening up about her anxiety.. Abi finally found the courage to explain her fears to Miss Gunther. "I want to know if my friends, Leila, Maya and Sada are safe. I wonder where they are. Whenever I watch the news,I see so many children dying in the boats and the camps that my mind cannot rest at nights. I dare not ask my parents anymore as they are busy making ends meet. I wonder if anyone can help me find them," she asked warily." Why did you not come to me earlier,Abi? You should not keep things bottled up, you know. You need to let us know what your problems are. We will try and sort them out for you. Well, let me see what I can do to locate your friends. But I cannot promise anything. You must assure me that you will not get disappointed if I cannot help you" said Miss Gunther in a firm but kind voice. Abi smiled wearily to herself. She had seen so many disappointments since the war that she had almost given up. She had lost her dear friends, her lovely school, her beautiful home and a perfect life. She had to say goodbye to her pets -Mirfat and Miriam and leave all her dreams behind. What could be more disappointing than this? It was only papa's eagerness and determination that had carried her so far. So many times she had broken down and cried herself to sleep in her dingy tent. But she could not explain all this to Miss Gunther, who was going out of her way to help them. Ameena, of course, shared Abi's fears and challenges all the way through and Abi was truly grateful for that.

It was weeks and weeks before Miss Gunther called Abi and Ameena to her room. The girls had almost given up all hope when they were asked to meet the counsellor in the computer lab. Miss Gunther asked both the girls to close their eyes." Open your eyes only when you hear voices", she said in a mysterious tone while she set up a conference call on her large computer. All of a sudden the girls heard a loud scream," HI,Abi, Hi Ameena, we missed you so much". Abi and Ameena could not believe what they saw. Miss Gunther had approached several agencies and spoken to various officials before she located Sada, Maya and Leila. Maya and Sada were in Switzerland and Leila managed to relocate to Greece. The girls were stunned to see their long lost friends waving madly at them and blowing kisses in the air with a startled treble in their voices which later developed into a high-pitched shout." Hi---Where were you all these days? Why did you not try to get in touch with us? Do you know how much we missed you"?, The girls' excited answers were jumbled and incoherent in their excitement to talk all at once.

All three of them had grown tall and thin. They looked happy and cheerful. Abi could not speak for a long time as the shock was too much to take.. She had never dreamt that she would ever see them again. After a while Miss Gunther left the room while the girls went back and forth talking about their old and new lives and discussing their siblings and their families." We will definitely meet you some time" said Abi with a new determination."I am sure Miss Gunther can arrange that too. Bye for now. I must rush home and tell papa and Amma about the good news",she said literally jumping up and down. She gave Ameena a warm hug and held her hand tightly. They rushed out and thanked Miss Gunther, tears welling up with gratitude and happiness. "Now take the day off and spend it with your parents and loved ones," said Miss Gunther.She realised that the girls were too happy and excited to concentrate on their classes for the rest of the day." Be back early tomorrow. I have arranged a trip to the zoo, the aquarium and the planetarium. The school will provide lunch and refreshments.Don't forget to get your permission letter signed by one of your parents. Now run off and celebrate". Miss Gunther chased the girls away to their homes, feeling very very satisfied with her secret successful mission. There was a special glow on her face too .

Abi and Ameena were in a dazed state after all this excitement. For the first time in four years Abi felt that their worst fears were over and that could start a new life all over aagin. They had a safe home, their parents were alright and they would grow up together with their dear, dear friends even if they were in different countries. They could speak to them and exchange notes whenever they wanted. Abi and Ameena hugged each other, danced round the trees and sang loudly. They were so breathless at the end of this grand, virtual reunion with their long lost friends, that they had to lie down on the grass in the park for a few minutes.. They could not simply believe their luck.

"We can have all the fun that we missed for so long" they prattled. "Let's break the good news to Amma and celebrate with samosas and sherbet" shouted Abi as she dragged Ameena to her apartment. Amma was thrilled with this wonderful piece of information and gave a special, tearful hug to both of them. The pure joy on the girls' faces was something that she would never forget for the rest of her life.

"Well, now that you have found your friends there is only thing missing in your life. Maybe you are going to get that too", said amma with a wink. "Look behind the door." Abi flung the door open and screamed out loudly. She saw a tiny cage with a parrot munching on a piece of carrot. "Today is the best day in my life I have got everything I wanted all at once" she screamed." What shall I name her?" Abi asked Ameena.

"MIrfat, of course" screamed the girls in unison, while Amma smiled to herself from behind the door. There was absolutely no doubt about that of course!

About the Author

Sreelatha Radhakrishnan

Sreelatha Radhakrishnan is a post-graduate in English Literature and worked as a faculty member, administartor and co-ordinator in a prestigous community college in Chennai, India. After her retirement, she started travelling and spending time with her grandchildren abroad. She realized that her story telling techniques were well appreciated and on her return started writing stories for children,. She has published two childrens' books and contributed several articles to prestigous dailies and magazines in South India.

www.ingramcontent.com/pod-product-compliance
Lightning Source LLC
LaVergne TN
LVHW041603070526
838199LV00047B/2117